Loving Lily
Kirsten Osbourne

Prologue

Lily was six when she met the boy she knew she would love for the rest of her life. Not many six year olds would recognize something like that, but Lily was more aware than most.

She'd sneaked off to run through the woods barefoot, which was her favorite springtime fun. Of course, her father didn't consider that a worthy pursuit for a young lady. He wanted her to spend her days in the nursery with her nanny, learning to embroider and act like a lady. He didn't much like her climbing trees either, but that had never stopped her.

Through the trees, she saw him, high atop his horse. He was with an older gentleman who she later learned was his father. He followed along after his father, but when his father got off his horse to speak with hers, he dismounted, and followed the trail into the woods instead.

When she saw him coming her way, she scurried up the nearest tree as agilely as any monkey. She sat on one of the branches just over the path and watched as he walked below her. If he'd looked up, he'd have seen her bare foot dangling over his head, but he didn't look up.

Lily had to cover her mouth to keep her giggles from being too loud, but still he heard her. He walked back to where she sat in the tree looking up at her. "Who're you?"

She had never talked to a strange boy before. She talked to her older brothers, of course, but they were off at Eton now. She didn't have much chance to leave their family's estate, so she rarely had the opportunity to talk to anyone to whom she wasn't related. Except the servants, of course. Not that she was complaining. She loved the area surrounding her home. It was a child's fantasy land.

She stared down at him for a moment and decided answering wouldn't hurt her. "I'm Lily. This is my family's land."

"Oh, my dad came here to see your dad then. He's the earl?"

She nodded. "Yeah. And Mama was the countess. She died, though. I killed her." She whispered the last words as if they were some sort of sinful secret.

"How'd you kill her?" he asked fascinated by this little girl. He was ten, and soon to be off to Eton, but he considered himself almost grown up compared to this little thing.

She shrugged. "I didn't mean to. It happened when I was born."

"Oh. That just happens sometimes. It's not your fault she died."

Lily's eyes widened. "It's not?"

He shook his head. "No. Did someone tell you it was your fault?"

"No, but they sometimes look at me like they blame me."

"I'm sure no one blames you." He looked up at her for a moment before asking, "Do you need help down from there?"

Lily looked around her. She climbed this tree all the time. She didn't need help. But he looked so strong, and willing. Maybe she should let him help her down. Her nanny was always telling her that gentlemen liked ladies who were helpless. "Yes, please."

She scooted across the branch to the trunk, and wrapped her arms around it like usual. She put her foot on the knot and scurried down. She was beside him before she remembered she was supposed to let him help her.

She gave him a perplexed look. "I'm sorry. I forgot to let you help. I can climb it again, so you can help me down!"

He laughed. "Nahh. It looks like you've got it figured out." He started walking deeper into the woods. "How come you're not up in the nursery? Are you supposed to be out here?"

She shook her head. "Papa would be very disappointed in me if he knew I was here. He thinks ladies should practice embroidery and always look perfect." She looked down at her bare feet. "And always wear shoes."

"Well, I don't think you're any less a lady than you would be with shoes on," he said courteously.

"Thank you!" She knew then she loved him. She wanted to marry him. Of course, she'd have to wait until she was older. Wait, could she marry a man whose name she didn't know? How could she tell Papa which man she wanted? "You never told me your name."

"Christopher. My brothers call me Kit." He liked the nickname, but his father wouldn't use it. Of course, Father wasn't very interested in him anyway. His oldest brother, Jack, was the heir. His brother Harold was the spare. He was the spare's spare, and no one needed a spare for their spare.

"May I call you Kit?"

"I'd like that." She was a funny little thing. She spoke as if she were already grown. Her red hair was braided and hung down her back. Her eyes were what really enchanted him, though. They were the same shade of green as the leaves.

"How many brothers do you have? I have two. They're at Eton now." She jabbered on as they walked.

"Two. The oldest, Jack, is at Cambridge. My other brother, Hal, is at Eton. I go to Eton next year," he added importantly.

"I don't get to go away to school. I hate being a girl sometimes." She kicked a rock out of her way as they wandered along.

He caught her arm. "You'd look awful funny in that dress if you were a boy," he told her. When she grinned up at him, he knew it had been the right thing to say. "We'd better turn around and go back. My father won't like it if he can't find me when it's time to go."

"I'm glad I met you." Was that a good way to tell him to come back when she was old enough to get married?

They walked silently for a while. Finally the house was within sight through the trees. "I have to go find my shoes and sneak back to the nursery before Nanny wakes up from her nap."

He grinned. "Is that how you got out?"

"That's how I get out every day." She held out her hand. "It was a pleasure meeting you." The words had been pounded into her head so many times she could never forget to say them.

He bowed over her hand, kissing her knuckles. "I hope to see you again, my lady."

She giggled softly. "I hope so too, Kit." She turned and ran in the direction of the servant's entrance. It was the only way to get in without being noticed. She sat on the floor and pulled her shoes on, running up the stairs.

She was sitting on her bed, playing with a porcelain doll she'd gotten for her birthday when Nanny woke up to check on her. Nanny didn't mention the dirt on her dress as she changed her. Just as she knew that Lily wouldn't mention her nap to her father.

Chapter One

JUNE 1811

Lily sat through the long process of having her hair fixed just right. Her father insisted it was time for her debut in a few months, but talked him into a small house party first. Not that she was nervous about her first season in London. It was just that she wanted to see if it could be avoided.

Kit should be finished with university this year. Maybe he would be there. He would sweep her off her feet, and Papa would agree there was no need for a season when she'd already found her true love. He'd offer a huge dowry, because as a third son, Kit would need it, and they would live happily ever after.

She hadn't seen him since that day in the woods, but she remembered him perfectly. He had hair that was so dark it was almost black and the warmest brown eyes she'd ever seen. What else did she really need to know?

"Ow! Be careful, Bernice. I want to have some hair left for the party," she joked. In truth, her maid had become her closest friend. She knew Papa would cringe if she ever said such a thing aloud, but there were no other young ladies around for her to befriend.

"I'm sorry, Lady Lily."

"We're alone! How many times do I have to tell you to drop the formalities when we're alone?"

"Sorry!"

"Are you almost finished?" Lily knew she should be more patient, but it wasn't in her nature. She couldn't stand sitting still and doing nothing. She'd still rather be running barefoot through the woods than anything else in the world.

Papa had finally asked his sister, Aunt Margaret, to come live with them. Margaret was a widow and a stickler for rules of propriety. Papa was certain Aunt Margaret could tame her. Lily sighed as she looked down at her hands. She may not have been tamed, but she certainly knew how to pretend she was.

"Yes. Your hair is going to look glorious!"

Lily smiled. It had to look perfect for Kit. She knew she shouldn't count on him coming, but she'd seen his father several times over the years as he'd come to do business with hers. Surely his family would be invited.

Finally, her hair finished, she stood to allow Bernice to help her into her dress. It was made of silk and a deep forest green. It matched her eyes perfectly. When she was dressed, she looked into the mirror and sighed. "Yes, that's just right." She turned and threw her arms around her maid. "Thank you! My hair is just like Mama's in the portrait in the hall."

"I'm glad you like it." Bernice hugged her back for a moment, and then walked in a slow circle around her, trying to be sure everything was just right. "Remember not to kick your shoes off."

Lily sighed. "I hate shoes. And these new slippers pinch my toes. My dress is so long, what difference would it make if I danced without them?"

Bernice laughed. "Your papa would have my head. You have to behave like a lady. Just this once!"

"I'll try." Lily looked down at the floor as she said the words. She knew she was the bane of her father's existence. He wanted her to be the perfect lady and marry well. She didn't care if she married well, as long as she married Kit.

Her father knocked on her door. "Are you ready, Lily?"

"Yes, Papa." She walked to the door and took his arm. Tonight she would be presented to the people at the small country dance her father had her aunt arrange. She walked as gracefully as possible to the top of the stairs.

They descended slowly. She kept her chin up the entire time as she'd been taught. Finally they reached the bottom, and he presented her to a young man who immediately took her arm and twirled her away in a dance.

She'd have to wait until she got to London and was given permission before she danced the waltz, but she'd had a dance teacher come to teach her all of the dances she could possibly be expected to dance, both here and in London.

She made small talk with the young man she danced with, trying to keep her eyes on his face to show she was interested in what he had to say, but her eyes were constantly searching the room. Was Kit here? Would she even be able to recognize him if he was? It had been twelve years since their first meeting. Surely, he would have changed in that time. She knew she had.

She curtseyed politely at the end of the dance and the young man returned her to her father. She thanked him sweetly for the dance.

Her father then presented her to the man she knew was Kit's father. "Lily, this is the Viscount Burgess."

She smiled. Were his sons with him? "I'd like you to meet my sons. This is Jack, my eldest."

Lily held out her hand for him to kiss. Jack looked faintly as if he could be related to Kit. "It's nice to meet you."

Jack nodded. "The pleasure is mine."

Viscount Burgess indicated the young man on his other side. "This is my second son, Harold."

"It's nice to meet you, Mr. Burgess." She held her hand out for him as well. She couldn't help but wonder if the brothers felt like they were kissing one another as they each kissed the same spot on her hand.

"And you, Lady Lily." His eyes met hers and she smiled. He had the same eyes as Kit.

She looked at the viscount expectantly waiting for him to introduce Kit. Was he here? "And are these your only sons?" Her father glanced at her reprovingly. She knew she shouldn't have said it, but she had to know if Kit was there.

"No, my third son is...where is Christopher anyway?" He turned to his eldest son to ask that.

"He's standing right behind you, Father." Jack gestured to the young man behind him.

"Ah, yes. Here we are. My third son, Christopher."

Lily raised her eyes expectantly. Did he remember her? She held her hand out to the man in question.

"Lady Lily. It's wonderful to meet you." His eyes danced as he brought her fingers to his lips. "Would you care to dance?"

Lily smiled. "I'd love to." He looked older, of course, but the laughter was still there in his chocolate eyes. She gripped the muscle of his arm through his black jacket, and knew she was holding him too tightly, but she didn't care. She was keeping this man. "I hoped you'd come," she whispered just loudly enough for him to hear.

He smiled. "I wouldn't have stayed away. I wasn't sure you'd remember me." He paused for a moment. "You were very young the first time we met."

"How could I forget you, Kit?" She paused for a moment, knowing that she should be making polite conversation when all she wanted to do was beg him to ask her father for her hand. "Are you finished with your studies now?"

"Finally! I won't say I didn't enjoy them, because I did, but I'm happy to be finished."

"What will you do now?" she asked.

He shrugged. "Honestly, I'm not entirely certain. I do hope to marry, though." He stared deep into her eyes as he said those words. "Soon."

She smiled. "Do you have a bride picked out then?" She only wanted one answer, of course. If he gave any other, she may very well throw a temper tantrum right there on the dance floor. She smiled to herself. Wouldn't her aunt and father be surprised at that?

He nodded, his eyes never leaving hers. "If she'll have me, of course. You see, I've known for years the kind of wife I wanted."

"Really? Tell me about her."

"Well, she has to have copper-colored hair. And forest-green eyes. And, this is the most important part." He leaned forward as if he were imparting a secret.

She felt herself drawn to him as if by a magnet. She leaned in for the last part. "What?"

"She must hate to wear shoes on warm spring days," he whispered.

She laughed aloud. "I tried to convince my aunt that I would be a more graceful dancer without slippers, and told her that I shouldn't wear them tonight." She flicked up the hem of her gown to show him the slippers that peeked out from under. "Alas....I lost that argument."

He chuckled. "Those don't look too terribly confining," he said.

"They pinch my toes. I hate shoes." She sounded so forlorn that he was tempted to get to his knees and remove her slippers right there and then.

He wished he could pull her to him for a kiss then, but knew it would never do. Not here. "Will you meet me tonight?"

She knew it wasn't proper. She knew the correct answer was a loud "no" and a dressing down. Instead she heard herself whisper, "What time and where?"

"In the woods, under the tree where I first met you. The party should be over at midnight, so shall we say one?"

She nodded. She knew she shouldn't, but she didn't care. This was Kit, and she was going to marry him.

They didn't dance together again that evening. It wouldn't have been proper, and with her father watching her so closely, she knew that propriety was important. She danced with all the young bachelors there, and even some of the older ones. She knew they were all interested in the generous dowry they expected her father to settle on her.

It was a long night, and the only thing that kept her going was the promise of stolen time with Kit at the end of it. Oh, she wouldn't have to have a London season after all. She'd be engaged before she had to go off and live in the hustle and bustle of the city. She was a country girl, and although Hyde Park sounded nice, there was nothing else the city had to offer that she wanted.

Bernice helped her undress at the end of the long evening. She had already picked out a day dress in her mind that she would wear when she sneaked out to meet Kit. Bernice left her all tucked up in her bed, feigning sleep.

As much as she trusted Bernice, Lily knew her friend was paid by her father. She couldn't trust her with a secret this big. She couldn't trust anyone with a secret this big.

After the door closed behind her maid, Lily counted to one-hundred slowly. She wanted to be sure she gave her enough time to come back in if she was going to. Finally, she flung the covers back and quickly threw off her nightgown. She flipped through her closet until she found the dress she wanted and slipped it over her head. She'd made sure to choose one that buttoned in the front so she wouldn't need help.

She was halfway down the backstairs when she realized that she'd forgotten her shoes. She still wore them as seldom as she could get away with. She laughed. Kit wouldn't mind. She walked quickly across the lawn and spotted him under the tree he had designated as their meeting place.

As soon as she saw him, she slowed her walk, watching him as he stood under the tree, waiting for her. His focus was on the tree limb above him, so he didn't see her as she approached. With her bare feet, she made no sound. Finally, she was close enough to touch him and did just that. Her hand reached out to his arm and gave it a light squeeze.

He turned to her with a smile, taking her hand and pulling her deeper into the woods. Finally, he stopped and turned to her, setting down the lantern he'd carried with him. "When was the last time you climbed that tree?" he asked nodding in the direction they'd come from.

She shrugged. "Last week, I think," she answered honestly. She smiled up at him sweetly. "I've outgrown climbing trees in my old age."

He pulled her into his arms slowly, his head lowering to hers. It was her first kiss, and she was eager for it. She pressed her lips to his and wrapped her arms around his shoulders. "Open your mouth," he whispered against her lips.

She gasped in surprise at his words, but it was enough. His head swooped down again and his tongue found entrance. His hands pulled her close against him, and she felt a jolt of surprise. Was it okay to kiss this way? Surely not. Her aunt had told her to let no man kiss her until after she was married, and then only her husband. Her aunt had set herself up as the moral gauge in Lily's life. Lily chose to ignore her whenever possible.

After a moment, he trailed his lips to her ear, whispering softly, "I want you to be my wife."

She clung to his shoulder tightly. "Talk to my father." She knew her father would accept Kit. He was a gentleman after all. And her father wanted her to be happy.

"Do you think he'd accept? Me being a third son and all?" He had no clue how he'd support a wife, but he didn't care. He had some money, and they could live with his family for a time. Whatever it took, as long as he had this woman by his side, he knew that life would be good.

He hadn't gone to the party planning to marry her. He wondered if she'd even remember him. He'd half expected to meet the pretty little girl from the woods, but in her place was a beautiful woman. He'd deliberately hidden himself behind her father so he could observe her unnoticed.

At first, he'd been certain her father had finally managed to crush her impish spirit, which had saddened him for reasons he couldn't explain. Then, he'd had to work to prevent himself from laughing when she'd demanded to know if his father had presented all of his sons. In truth, his father probably wouldn't have gotten around to introducing him. He was a third son, after all, and not expected to marry well at all.

When he'd stepped forward and taken her hand, he'd known that the happy little hoyden who'd been certain she killed her mother still lived in the well-groomed lady. He knew then, without a shadow of a doubt, that he wanted to marry the lady and raise many more wild little girls who would know their own minds and hate being locked up in the nursery.

After a moment, when she hadn't answered, he asked again. "Will your father skewer me alive for daring to ask for his precious daughter's hand?"

She laughed. "I think he'll be happy to be rid of me. As long as I'm not marrying the stable lad, of course." He'd actually probably be relieved that he was able to get her married off so easily.

He looked grim in the moonlight shining through the branches of the trees overhead. "I'm not the stable lad, but I am a third son. I don't have a title to offer you."

She shrugged, truly not caring what he had or who he was. As far as she was concerned, he was Kit and that was good enough for her. They could live in a tree house for all she cared. She'd probably even like it, she thought with a grin. "I don't care one whit about a title. I just want a man who will love me for who I am."

"That, I will do!"

He kissed her one last time, and then picked up the lantern. "We need to get you back up to the manor. We don't want anyone to notice you're missing."

She sighed. "I would rather spend the entire night out here with you." She could picture them sleeping on a blanket under the stars. His arms would stay wrapped around her all night long.

He would have liked that as well, but for reasons other than what she was thinking. "Soon, we'll be able to do that. I'll talk to your father soon." He smiled down at her, trying hard to believe she was interested in marriage to him.

She stopped in her tracks. "Please kiss me one more time, so I won't think I'm dreaming."

He laughed, set the lantern down carefully, and pulled her into his arms. "I would never want you to think you were dreaming, love." His lips descended again. This time she needed no coaxing. She opened her mouth to allow his tongue entrance, and met it with her own. Her hands rubbed his shoulders through the back of his shirt.

When he finally lifted his head, they were both breathing hard. "I don't know how I'll ever be able to wait until the wedding night," he whispered against her lips.

She smiled. She wasn't sure exactly what happened on a wedding night, but she'd seen enough animals mating to have a pretty good idea. It didn't look pleasant, but if it made him happy, she would participate.

They walked again through the woods, and he stopped under the tree where they'd met so many years before. "Will you meet me here again? Tomorrow night?"

"Of course I will!" Her aunt had always told her that a lady didn't show too much enthusiasm when being pursued by a gentleman. Lily didn't care. This wasn't just any man, this was Kit. She wasn't going to put on airs and pretend to be someone she was not.

They kissed again, just a brief brush of his lips against hers in farewell, and she dashed across the lawn to the backstairs. Once she was again tucked into her bed, she slept deeply, dreaming of little boys with jet black hair and chocolate brown eyes.

Chapter Two

EVERY NIGHT FOR TWO weeks, they slipped into the woods to meet. Every night, they talked about everything they could think of. His words painted a picture of a lonely little boy who had grown into a happy young man once he was out from beneath his father's thumb and away at school.

She talked about the hours and hours of "lady practice" as she thought of it. Her aunt had made her stop everything she enjoyed. She had spent hours at the pianoforte, even though she'd known from the beginning she had a tin ear. She'd been forced to practice water colors, and even she couldn't tell what she'd painted at the end.

She laughed about one painting her aunt had declared a beautiful likeness of the forest near her home. She didn't have the heart to tell her it was meant to be the dining table.

Kit had smiled at all of her stories, drinking in the sight of her. All of his years of loneliness were obliterated by the sound of her voice. It wasn't her beauty that drew him, although she was beautiful. It was the utter simplicity of her. She had no desire to be anyone she wasn't. She was herself and she was happy.

"I'm so glad I've found you," he told her late one night as they walked hand in hand through the trees.

"You never lost me," she whispered. "I've been right here waiting for you th whole time."

He smiled. "I want to speak to your father tomorrow. To ask for your hand." He quickly dropped to one knee on the forest floor. "Will you marry me, Lily, and make me the happiest man in all of England?"

She frowned. "Only England? Not all the world? What have I been doing wrong?"

He laughed softly. "In all the world. I didn't want you to think I was being too melodramatic."

"Some situations call for melodrama. Of course, I'll marry you, and make us the happiest couple in all the universe."

He stood and gathered her into his arms. "The universe? Is that a touch too melodramatic?"

She shook her head adamantly. "Not when it's the truth."

He laughed, dipping his head for a kiss. He knew she wanted to be married soon, the same as he did, so she wouldn't draw things out much. "Do you think two months is enough time to plan the wedding?"

She shrugged. "Three days would be enough for me. I don't need a huge wedding. As long as you're the man by my side, I'll be happy as a clam."

He frowned. "How do you know clams are happy? Have you stuck your head in the ocean and listened for their laughter? Do you ever wonder where those expressions come from?"

"I know there's not a clam alive who is as happy as I am right this minute. I can't wait to be your wife, Kit."

He pressed a kiss to the top of her head. "I'll come by in the morning and talk to your father."

She smiled and nodded. "I'll be waiting for you."

THE FOLLOWING MORNING found Lily sitting in front of her window watching for Kit. When she saw him arrive on his horse, she called Bernice to make sure her hair was still just right. She wore one of her best day dresses. She wanted to look perfect for Kit.

Bernice knew she was expecting a man to propose, but had no idea she'd been meeting him on the sly. She refused to put Bernice in a situation where she'd have to choose between being loyal to a close friend and lying to her employer.

"Are you excited? I know you weren't looking forward to going to London for the Season." Bernice stood behind her with a hairbrush, taking down the hair she'd mussed as she nervously waited, so she could redo it completely.

"Excited and nervous, and oh so happy. Papa should be sending for me any moment. Kit's here now. I saw him ride up."

Bernice smiled down at her friend. It was good to see her so happy.

THE MEETING WITH HER father didn't go at all as Kit had planned.

The Earl of Marsgate simply laughed in his face and told him that he'd never allow his daughter to marry the third son of a Viscount. Maybe the second son of a Duke, but never would she marry so far beneath her.

"She came to me this morning and talked about you coming here to offer for her," he added.

Kit looked up from his hands which he was wringing together in his lap. "She did?" His eyes lit up with hope.

"She told me to make sure you knew she couldn't marry so far beneath her, but it was nice to have her first proposal out of the way. It will make it so much easier to start her Season in London."

Kit had planned on trying to see Lily, even if his offer was refused, before leaving the estate, but found he couldn't do that. He took his leave and went home to pack his belongings.

He was hurt by her decision. He knew most women would feel that way, but he hadn't expected Lily to change her mind and not even be willing to talk to him about it herself. Why wasn't she willing to face him?

A third son had only two real options in life. He could either become a vicar, or he could join the military. He spoke with his father about the latter option. His father immediately agreed to purchase a commission for him. He was certain his father figured if he was off on the continent fighting Boney, then he would be out of his hair. And he would be able to forget about Lily.

WHEN LILY WAS CALLED into her father's study the day after the party, she tried to keep the smile from her face. She knew that Kit must have offered for her, and she was ready to see him. She'd had Bernice fix her hair in an elegant style, and she made certain to wear slippers instead of running through the house barefoot.

She knocked on the door to his study and smoothed her dress. She pinched her cheeks to give them a bit more color. Was Kit in there with her father?

At her father's command, she opened the door and stepped inside. The room was empty but for her father, so she took the seat he indicated and waited for him to speak.

"A young gentleman came to speak with me this morning," he began. "Do you know the gentleman I'm speaking of?" He drummed his fingers against his desk as he asked.

She nodded. "Yes, Papa." Where was he? Maybe he was waiting outside for her so they could begin to plan the wedding. She did her best to keep the huge grin from her face. She was going to be married to the man she loved.

"He asked me to let you know that he'd reconsidered his offer. He would rather hold out for an heiress with a greater fortune than you possess."

Her face fell. That couldn't be true. "We must be talking about different gentleman. The one I'm thinking of would never say that." Kit would want to marry her no matter what her fortune was. He wasn't after her money. He loved her for who she was on the inside, not for the money from her dowry. He'd never spoken to her of money. If he cared about it so much, he would have mentioned it at least in passing.

"Christopher Burgess? He's a third son. Of course, he can't marry unless you come with a fortune. Now, your dowry is a fortune by some standards, but obviously not by his. I'm sorry, daughter." He didn't look sorry. He had a half smile on his face as he said the words.

"What did you say to him to make him leave, Papa? He never would have done so if you hadn't said something." She knew he wouldn't. Kit would be true to her. True, she'd only known him for a short while, but she knew him. She knew his soul, and knew it was bound to hers. What had her father done?

He folded his arms across his chest. "I told him the amount of your dowry, and he chose to find a wealthier bride. That is all."

Lily nodded slowly. "Yes, Father." She stood and left the room. Whatever he said to her, she knew Kit wouldn't give up on her because her dowry wasn't enough.

She went to her room and sat down on her bed. There were no tears to be cried. She wrote Kit a letter, explaining what her father had said, and telling him of her feelings, and how she would always be true. She couldn't send it without her father's knowledge, so she put it in a frilly little box meant for jewelry she'd received as an eighteenth birthday gift. She would give it to him the next time she saw him.

Chapter Three

The Season was finally over, and Lily was on her way back to Devon to Marsgate Manor. After four long Seasons of trying *not* to find a husband, she was ready to be a country girl again. She looked over at Bernice sound asleep on the seat opposite her. Bernice would be happy to be home as well.

She watched out the window as the countryside passed by. They'd been traveling for days, having spent the past three nights in various inns along the way. James, her second brother, was riding alongside the family's coach. He refused to stay cooped up the entire time, but didn't feel it was safe for her to travel with just her maid.

In London, her brothers pretty much left her to her own devices. She lived with her aunt, but as long as Bernice was with her, her aunt ignored her. She made sure she lived the life she should.

After their father's death three and a half years ago, she'd made an arrangement with her eldest brother, Charles, regarding her time spent husband-hunting in London. If, after her fourth Season, she hadn't found a man she wanted to marry, then she wouldn't have to go back. She was also given the final say in whether or not she'd accept a man. The arrangement was scandalous, according to her aunt, but she didn't care.

She'd had more than her share of proposals, but none had been Kit, so she'd had her brother turn down each and every one of them. She would marry Kit, or she'd be a spinster for the rest of her days.

In the years they'd been apart, she hadn't heard from Kit even once. She wasn't sure what her father had said to him when he'd come to propose, but she was more than willing to work through whatever issues there could be between them. She missed him every day, and would wait for him forever if she needed to.

She was on her way home to Marsgate, and this time she was going home for good. She would no longer have to spend half the year in London. Instead, she could stay in the country where she belonged. Until Charles chose a wife of his own, she would play hostess for him. It was a good arrangement for them both.

Charles was already thirty, and was neglecting his duty to the family by not choosing a wife, but he just wasn't interested yet. When he was in London, he spent his time in parliamentary pursuits, instead of looking for a bride. He wasn't yet ready to marry, and he was going to wait until he was. Now that Father wasn't around to insist they all do as he wanted, they each did as they pleased. The freedom Lily had when she was in their country home would have caused most mamas of young girls to have a case of the vapors.

She looked down at the letter she was writing. She'd written letters to Kit every day since he'd left her life. She kept him apprised of the details of her days, and talked about the way she felt about him. How she knew she'd never marry if he wasn't there. She spoke of how much she missed him, and worried about him. She'd learned long ago that he was fighting the French in the cavalry.

She quickly finished the letter, and stared out the window once more. Now that Napolean had finally been defeated, she hoped Kit would soon be home.

She tucked the letter into her valise and watched as Marsgate Manor came into view. Finally. She wouldn't be forced to leave again until Kit came home and made her his wife. Was he back in England yet? Would he immediately leave the cavalry, or would he stay on the continent for a while?

She wondered how the small orphanage she'd spent the last few years helping had fared during her long absence. As soon as she was home, she would ride over, and see if they needed anything.

She didn't bother to change into her riding habit, simply walked straight to the stables and asked that her mare, Snowball, be saddled. Snowball, a pure white mare, had been a birthday gift for her tenth birthday. She liked to spend several hours a day with the children whenever she was home.

Looking down, she realized she was still wearing her traveling dress. It was of the latest fashion, and something she would usually never consider wearing to help with the orphans, but it didn't matter if it was ruined. She would no longer need her traveling gowns. She was going to spend the rest of her life rusticating in the country. How glorious that sounded!

She quickly mounted her horse, detesting the side saddle. She couldn't ride astride in this gown, though. She raced through the trees, finally happy. She was home.

The ten minute ride to the orphanage flew by. She couldn't believe she was actually home to stay. As she neared, she heard a shout go up from some of the children. They raced over to her.

She quickly dismounted and spread her arms wide. Many of the children ran to her. One little girl held up her doll to Lily. She took it and gazed at it. "Oh no! Her dress has been torn! I'm so sorry, Mary."

Mary, only about six, sniffled and nodded. "No one has time to fix it, milady. Poor Caroline will grow cold."

"May I take her home with me tonight? I promise to bring her back first thing in the morning." She knew that Bernice would be happy to fix it. Her maid usually accompanied her on her frequent trips to the orphanage, but she needed to see to Lily's unpacking, and Lily wasn't willing to wait. In London, she'd never have been allowed to go alone, but here in the country, no one would think twice about it.

Mary nodded regally. "Thank you."

Lily carefully stowed the doll in her saddle bag. "I will ask Bernice to make her presentable. She will be happy to do it, Mary."

Mary skipped off toward the house, happy to have found someone willing to take their time with her most precious possession. They'd known it was almost time for Lady Lily to return, and with her return, the children knew their lives would improve.

Lily and Bernice had made each little girl at the orphanage her own rag doll. Bernice had sewn the clothes, because Lily still had no patience for needle work. Lily had stuffed each doll and sewn it closed. She had been happy to do something to help the children she loved so much.

They had also made sure that each little boy had some sort of toy. Usually a small toy soldier or a carved wooden pony. She had found most second hand, hand-me-downs from children of aristocrats, but had purchased a few of them new. All that mattered was that each child had something to call his own.

Mrs. Brown, the matron of the home, clapped her hands together briskly. "It's time for luncheon."

Lily walked over to speak with Mrs. Brown while the children washed their hands for the evening meal. "Is everything all right?" She was thrilled to see her friend after so many months away. Part of her agreement with Charles had included her not coming home at all during the Season. She had to focus all her time and attention on the parties and balls that would lead her to marriage.

Mrs. Brown nodded. "Now that we have both you and Viscount Burgess helping us, it will work out well."

Lily had heard a couple of years back about the death of Kit's father, so this must be his eldest brother, Jack. "Is he helping financially then?" The idea thrilled Lily. She had given all her pin money to the orphanage for years, and had pestered Charles until he'd committed a monthly sum, but still, it was never enough.

"Financially and physically. He comes here at least one afternoon per week and does some of the manual labor. He has done some hunting for our table, and even gone out and chopped wood for our stove. I've never known a lord to be willing to do so much for orphans."

Lily was clearly surprised. She hadn't gotten to know Jack, but he'd hardly seemed the type to worry about those less fortunate. "That's wonderful! How long has he been helping?"

"Only about a month, milady, but he assures us that it will continue."

Lily smiled. "I certainly hope it does. I will be sure to thank him when I see him. I'm glad that your funding has increased." Glad was too mild a word for what she felt. She would do anything to help the orphans, but her brother held the purse strings. It would be wonderful to be able to help more children. More money would open up a whole new level of charity.

Mrs. Brown's face lit up. "It has increased so much we'll be able to afford the addition we've been needing. We won't have to turn any more children away."

Lily frowned. "I wasn't aware you'd turned any children away. You should have come to me, and I would have found a way to get more money for you." She would have moved to the servants quarters and put up four or five of the children in her room if she'd needed to.

"I knew you would, but you already give so much of yourself to the children. Both time and money." She studied her face. "Are you home for good now?"

"Yes, I am. I gave my brother the four Seasons I'd promised him. I'll be available to help from now on. Just send someone to the manor, and I'll come." She followed Mrs. Brown into the house and helped serve lunch to the children. When she'd first come to help at the orphanage, Mrs. Brown had protested everything she'd wanted to do to help. She felt a lady was above the menial tasks necessary for the upkeep of the house, but now she took it all in stride.

After their lunch, Lily helped Mrs. Brown get the younger children down for their naps. The older girls saw to the cleaning of the large house and the boys toiled in the garden that fed them most of the year.

After the children were down for their nap, Lily descended the stairs behind Mrs. Brown, planning to spend a couple of quiet hours helping her darn socks and go through the children's clothing to see what could be salvaged and what couldn't. It was time to start thinking about clothing for the fall and winter months.

The children generally went barefoot all through the summer months, but they needed to start now preparing for the long months ahead. Shoes and socks were essential as well as coats. The hours of work on the clothing, both sorting and finding who would be able to wear what seemed insurmountable at this point, but this was her fourth year to help.

After Kit had left four years ago, she'd wandered the area day after day. When she'd happened upon the orphanage, she'd found her true calling in life. Helping others was something she was made for.

Lily had been teaching the children in the fall, but right after Christmas every year, she'd had to go to London. This year, she'd be able to teach them the full nine months they needed instruction. She would have the children up to scratch in no time.

As soon as they reached the bottom of the stairs, Lily heard a shout from the boys working outside. She stepped out to see what the commotion was. A gentleman on a horse stopped and dismounted, asking two of the larger boys if they'd enjoy going hunting with him. "We could get some deer for the table tonight."

Mrs. Brown led Lily down the front porch steps and to the man. "Milord, I'd like you to meet the lady I've told you about. Lady Lily from Marsgate."

Lily smiled up at the man on the horse and her world started spinning. "Kit?" she said in a whisper. But he wasn't the Viscount Burgess now was he? Had both of his brothers died?

Chapter Three

HE INCLINED HIS HEAD slightly and turned to Mrs. Brown as if she hadn't spoken his name. "Is it all right if I borrow Johnny and Sammy? I'd loikve to bring you back some food for your table this evening."

Lily stared at him. Why was he being so cold to her? She knew he recognized her, or if not her at least her name. She had matured over the years he'd been gone. She was no longer a very young lady ready to begin her life among the ton.

"That would be wonderful, milord. I'll have two of the older girls take their place in the garden this afternoon," Mrs. Brown said with a smile for him. Mr. Brown would take the boys out on occasion, but he hadn't had time since the renovations had begun. It was a rare treat for them to go out with a member of the nobility.

Kit stalked off with the two boys. He'd brought muskets and made sure each boy had one. They all set off into the woods. Kit didn't look in her direction even once.

Lily turned to Mrs. Brown. "Was that the Viscount Burgess you mentioned before?" He must be, but how? Had Kit lost his entire family since she'd last seen him? Her heart went out to the boy she'd known.

"Oh, yes. I don't know why he was so rude to you. I've never seen him behave quite so abruptly."

Lily looked down. "He was supposed to offer for me once, when I was barely eighteen. My father said he came and asked about my dowry, but it wasn't enough so he changed his mind. I don't believe Kit would have done such a thing, but I never had a chance to talk to him and tell him that. He left for the war the following day." She paused a moment, looking at her hands as they twisted in front of her. "I assumed you meant Kit's older brother was helping."

Mrs. Brown touched Lily's shoulder comfortingly. Normally she would have never dared touch a member of the nobility, but she considered Lily a friend, and knew Lily felt the same about her. "You should talk to him. He seems quite alone."

Lily nodded. "He was a third son. He must have lost his father and both brothers since I last saw him." She didn't know for certain what had happened to Kit in the years they'd been apart, but there was no doubt in her mind he needed her. She'd seen sadness in his eyes during the brief moment he'd allowed them to meet hers.

"He told me that his eldest brother had died, killed by highwaymen. His second brother was very ill and died shortly after. His second brother died the same day Waterloo was fought."

Lily sighed. She hated that Kit had faced so much loss in such a short time. "I'll try to talk to him later." She took a deep breath. "Let's go through the children's clothes. I brought several outfits that my friends' younger siblings had outgrown from London. They're always happy to share what won't be used again."

Mrs. Brown smiled. "You have very generous friends. Of course, they'd probably be shocked if they saw our boys and girls wore their fine clothing for chores around the orphanage, but we're happy to take whatever we can."

They went inside and began the long task of sorting through the clothes, deciding what was good enough to be mended, and what must go into the rag pile.

KIT HAD BEEN STARTLED to see Lily at the orphanage. He'd been careful not to listen to any information about her family, wanting to know nothing about her. He'd assumed by what was said the woman helping the orphanage was her older brother's wife. He would have thought Lily would have married long ago.

Even after four years of war, he'd not been able to close his eyes without seeing her beautiful face in front of him. Her rejection still hurt to this very day. He wasn't happy to see her at all. He would rather go the rest of his days without seeing the lying debutante.

"No, Johnny. You have to steady the musket with your left hand and shoot with your right," he instructed, showing the lad how to hold the gun. "Mrs. Brown won't be happy with me if I stole her workers away and we don't bring home any fresh meat for supper."

Maybe he could work something out with her. He would make sure he went to the orphanage on a specific day every week, and she would stay away that day. That would work out nicely for both of them, since he was certain she didn't want to see him any more than he wanted to see her. He'd talk to her after they bought dinner back to the house.

Surely she could see they needed him as much as they needed her. The children only got to eat meat when he went out and shot it for them. They simply didn't have the resources for it. He couldn't help but remember all the orphans he'd seen while he'd been fighting. They reminded him so much of himself. Wanted by no one, but tolerated by all. He couldn't take in all the orphans in England, but he could make a difference with these few.

Not two hours later, he returned to the house with four plump pheasants. That would feed them all nicely for tonight, and even for breakfast in the morning. He dreaded having to have a conversation with Lily after the way she'd treated him, but he didn't see a way around it.

Mrs. Brown saw them coming and smiled her thanks. "That will make a wonderful stew for the children. Thank you, milord." She took the dead birds from him and immediately set to plucking them for their meal.

Kit looked around for Lily. Had she already left? He'd seen her horse as he'd passed by, so probably not. Where could she be?

He followed the sound of voices up the stairs and peeked into one of the children's bedrooms. The beds were all lined up against a wall. The older girls were sitting quietly on one of the beds while Lily described in detail a London ball. The girls hung on her every word.

He couldn't believe she would be so thoughtless as to describe something forever out of their reach. He stood and watched as the girls' faces lit up with the story.

"And did you find a husband there, milady? Will you be marrying and leaving us?" A girl of about fourteen asked the question. She was a beauty. Her hair was so blond it was almost white and her eyes were a pure sky blue.

Lily shook her head and laughed. "No. Do you want to know a secret?" she asked leaning forward. All the girls leaned toward her nodding. "I wasn't really looking for a husband. I just told my brother I was."

One of the girls gasped in shock. "Whyever not? Don't you want to marry? And have children?"

Lily sighed. "Of course, I do. I want that as much as any other woman. But I found the love of my life and he left me. I don't want any other but him."

Kit listened stiffly. So she'd found the love of her life, had she? And he'd left her? Good. It was no more than she deserved after the way she'd treated him. He went back down the stairs to wait for her. They needed to talk about schedules.

"Tell us about him, milady! How could someone leave someone as good and kind and beautiful as you?"

Lily shook her head sadly. "That's not a story for today, I'm afraid." The girls all nodded, obviously disappointed. Lily's life was so different from theirs they loved to hear about it. It was almost like having a fairy tale princess who came to visit them on a regular basis. "I think I heard the boys come back. We need to go down and help Mrs. Brown prepare supper."

The girls all stood and went down the stairs. The blond who'd been hanging on her every word stopped and touched her dress with one finger. "Your dress is the most beautiful I've ever seen," she whispered.

"Thank you, Megan. Would you like it? We could cut it down for you. I won't be needing it any longer. I'm a country lady again. There's no need for most of my fancy clothes."

Megan's whole face lit up. "Oh yes, milady."

The dress was made of cotton, and a forest green color, so it should wear well for the girl. Lily was happy to share some of her pretty clothes with the young girls.

She followed Megan down the stairs to the kitchen. There, she rolled up her sleeves and set the table for dinner. She had helped bake the bread for the meal earlier, and had even spent an hour peeling vegetables for the stew.

Kit saw her walk into the kitchen and followed. He stopped short when he saw her with her sleeves rolled up working. He'd expected her to do no more than tell stories to the children. He never thought she would pitch in and do the work. Especially not in the beautiful gown she was wearing. Was she not worried about ruining it? And why would she go to the orphanage in such a gown anyway? To show the children how much above them she was?

Once dinner was prepared, both were invited to eat with the children. Kit shook his head. "No, I have dinner waiting for me at home." He turned and walked out the door to see to the saddling of his horse.

Lily smiled. "I appreciate your kind offer, but I must go home. I haven't even seen my eldest brother yet."

Mrs. Brown looked shocked. "You should have gone to see your brother before coming to us!" She waved her hands toward the open door. "Go home to your brother!"

Lily laughed. "I knew he fared well during my absence. I saw him in London just two weeks ago. I didn't know how you'd done. I needed to see for myself." She rolled her sleeves down, smiling at young Mary who was standing beside her. "I'll be back in the morning with Caroline decently clothed."

Mary smiled. "Thank you. I shall miss her terribly while she is gone."

Lily took those words for what they were. A demand to have Caroline's clothes fixed tonight, so she could be returned to her owner as soon as humanly possible.

Lily waved to the children and left, going into the yard to ask Mr. Brown to saddle her horse. He had already done so, knowing that she would never take food from the orphans. On days she spent the entire day with them, she always brought her own lunch, knowing their food didn't stretch very far.

She took the reins and accepted his leg up. "Thank you, Mr. Brown. I shall see you tomorrow." She smiled down at him from her perch atop the horse.

She pulled the reins and guided her horse through the path in the woods toward home, mentally cursing the side-saddle. She took the path slowly, happy to be home once again. Every day, while in London, she got up early to ride through Hyde Park. It was the only thing that kept her sane during her time there. She'd had to be trailed by a groom the entire way, but it was better than no time spent in nature at all.

She was halfway home when Kit rode up beside her. "We need to talk, Lily." His voice sounded harsh to her ears.

She nodded, slowing her mare even more. "Yes, we do." *I missed you. I love you. I'm so glad you're home.*

"I want to set up a schedule for when we go to the orphanage so that we don't keep crossing paths. I'll go on Wednesdays, and you can go whenever you want, as long as it's not a Wednesday," he told her. "I find I can only carve out one day per week form my duties."

She stopped her mare entirely at that. "But why? Now that you're home, we can see each other. I've missed you so much, Kit." She knew the love was there on her face, and she didn't try to hide it. Why would she? He was all she'd ever wanted in this world, and now he was home. Her father was no longer alive to object to their marriage. It was time they were finally together.

He laughed. "Now that I have a title, I'm suddenly good enough for you? Is that it?" His warm chocolate colored eyes seemed to pierce right through her. She sighed.

She shook her head. "Of course not. I never cared if you had a title." Her brow furrowed as she said the words. Had that been what her father had said to frighten him away? "Did my father tell you I was holding out for a title?"

"As if you don't know. It's what you told him to tell me." Why was she acting as if she had no clue what had happened between her father and him four years ago? "I left because you wanted me to go. I deserved the common decency of you telling me yourself."

"No, Kit. Listen to me. It's not what I wanted. I would have married you and lived wherever happily. As long as I could be with you. I love you. My father told me you said my dowry wasn't enough, and told him to tell me you were no longer interested when you heard what it was." She took a deep breath. "I knew it for the lie it was instantly. I knew you wouldn't betray me, Kit."

"That's a good story. How long have you been working on it? Since you found out my brothers had died and the title was mine now?"

She drew in a shocked breath. He really had believed everything her father had said. "How could you even think it? I always knew you'd come back for me. I was certain my father had lied to you in some way to get you to leave me, but I never guessed it was anything so cruel. I'm sorry he said I wanted a title. I've spent the last four years in London trying *not* to find a husband. My brother and I made an arrangement. I only had to try to find someone for four Seasons. Now my Seasons are over, I'm home for good. I never wanted anyone but you."

He snorted. "You've never cared for anyone but yourself." He paused for a moment trying to calm his temper. He refused to believe what she said was true. If it was, he'd wasted four years hating her, and he refused to believe he could have done it. "Will you agree to the Wednesdays?"

She shook her head. "No, I won't. I refuse to avoid you, Kit. I want to be around you. I want you in my life. Why would I agree when I've waited four long years for you to come home." She knew she sounded belligerent and she just didn't care. She loved him, and she was going to make him see how happy they could be together if it killed them both.

"You don't want to make me angry, Lily."

She shrugged. "Why not? You would never hurt me. You love me." Her voice was confident. No matter what her father had done to keep them apart, she knew they were meant for each other. He couldn't hurt her any more than he could hurt the children at the orphanage.

He shook his head. "Your words killed my love years ago."

"My father's words bruised your love. It's not dead. It couldn't be. Not if it was as strong as mine." Her gaze met his, challenging him to disagree with her.

He wouldn't dignify that with an answer. "I'm going back to my house now. Please don't go to the orphanage on Wednesdays."

"Kit? If you don't love me, why don't you show me? Kiss me, and prove to me you don't still love me." She'd never been so bold with another man. Only Kit brought out that side of her. She'd never even allowed one of the gentlemen in London to kiss her. In her mind and heart she'd belonged to Kit since she was a little girl.

He stared at her for a moment. "Fine. When I kiss you, and you see I no longer feel anything for you, you'll avoid the orphanage on Wednesdays?"

She shrugged. She wasn't going to agree to that. "If you feel nothing for me, what difference does it make? Why don't you want to see me if you feel nothing? What does it matter?"

He threw his leg over his horse and dismounted, walking to her and holding his hands up to help her down. "Were you always this stubborn?" he asked.

"Absolutely. It's one of my better qualities." She placed her hands on his shoulders and gave him her full weight, completely trusting in him.

He grabbed her by the hips and pulled her to him roughly. His mouth lowered to hers. He couldn't stand to listen to her for another minute. Her voice had the same effect on him it had four years ago. He couldn't stop thinking of her as it was. Seeing her every week would be the end of him.

Her lips parted automatically for his kiss. Her arms would around his back to pull him closer. She pressed her entire body against him, wanting there to be nothing between them. She loved this man, and she wasn't giving up without a fight. She'd been denied so many things she wanted in life, but this was the only thing that truly mattered. She would not be denied Kit's love.

He groaned and pulled her even closer, his hands massaging her bottom through her dress and pulling her hips into contact with him. Why did he still want her so badly it felt as if his life depending on making love with her? He hated her. Didn't he?

She tugged his shirt out of his riding breeches and slid her hands against his bare skin. Never had she done anything so brazen, but she didn't care. Her fingers combed through the hair on his chest. Her mouth never losing contact with his.

She slowly unbuttoned his shirt, not wanting her access to him to be limited in any way. Once it was undone, she pushed it off and onto the forest floor. She broke the kiss off to trail her lips across his shoulder. She had no clue what she was doing, but she was certain he did. That was all that mattered.

His fingers went to the back of her dress and he unbuttoned it all the way down her back. She wasn't wearing a corset, thank God, so he pushed the dress down around her waist. He pulled her petticoat out of the way and lowered his head to her rigid nipple. He licked it for a second, and then sucked it straight into his mouth.

She let out a loud moan. She'd had no idea a man would do such a thing to her, but she found she enjoyed it immensely. She felt a heat rising between her legs. What did it mean?

He reached over to his horse, and pulled the blanket out of his saddle bag. He hadn't emptied his saddle bags since coming home from the war, not wanting to remember what had happened on the continent. He spread the blanket out onto the ground and lowered Lily onto the blanket descending on top of her.

"Is this what you want?" he asked against her lips.

"I want you, Kit. Nothing more and nothing less." She knew what she was doing was wrong. She didn't care. She loved this man, and if this is what it took to convince him her love was forever, then she would have relations with him in the woods. She'd do anything to make sure she kept him with her for the rest of her life.

That was good enough for him. His lips pressed to hers again, more demanding and more frantic all at once. He lay between her spread thighs with her dress and his breeches between them. He knew she'd never been with a man, but at that moment, he didn't care.

He rolled to her side for long enough to raise her skirt above her waist and to unfasten his breeches. He moved back over her and settled into the notch between her thighs. "This may hurt a bit," he warned her just as he slid inside her.

Lily was shocked by the feeling of fullness. She gasped slightly. There was some pain, but compared to the wonder of being one with Kit, it was of no matter.

Once he was inside, he held himself still for a moment, waiting for her to grow accustomed to him. Slowly he began moving in and out in the age-old dance of bodies. He watched her face carefully for any signs of pain, and seeing none, he drove them to fulfillment. Her sweet cries filled the air around them.

They lay together, limbs entangled for what could have been minutes or hours, Lily didn't know which. She turned to him, and kissed his lips.

"That was beautiful," she whispered. Her hand trailed along his chest. She felt what they'd done together had given her license to do anything she wanted to him.

Kit slowly came back to earth looking over at Lily with her hair spread out all around her, looking even more beautiful than he'd ever seen her. What had he been thinking? He rolled away from her and got dressed, helping her up and fastening the back of her gown for her.

Without saying a word, he gave her a leg up onto her horse. "You need to go home, Lily." His voice sounded hard and stilted.

She smiled. "I'll see you tomorrow, then."

He gave her a questioning look. "No. I won't be going to the orphanage tomorrow." Why did she think he'd be seeing her so soon?

"Not at the orphanage. When you come over to ask my brother for my hand." She gave him a loving look as she said the words. She could already see their beautiful sons and daughters.

He threw back his head and laughed. "Is that what this was all about? You really thought you could force me into offering for you?"

She stared at him in shock. "But....You love me. We couldn't have done that together if you hadn't loved me." He really wasn't going to offer for her? She hadn't maneuvered him into sex to get him to ask her to marry him. It was just something that had happened.

"Physical attraction is called lust, not love. Go home, Lily."

She spurred her horse on, the tears blinding her as she rode toward Marsgate Manor. How could she love someone so cold? He wasn't the Kit she loved, but she knew he was still in there. She'd find him if it took her the rest of her life to do so.

Kit watched her go, sadness filling his face. He did still love her. She was right about that. How he wished, he'd never agreed to touch her. Now he would have these memories tormenting him for the rest of his days. He loved her, but he could never trust her. He mounted his horse and headed home. His mind on the beautiful woman he loved, but would never allow himself to have.

Chapter Five

LILY FELL INTO A PATTERN in the months that followed. She spent every day but Sunday with the orphans as she always had. She was cordial to Kit when he was there, but she never again talked about loving him.

Every time she went, Bernice was now with her. Bernice brought her sewing kit and dug into the clothing problem with a vengeance. Lily donated many of her old gowns, and brought the clothing her friends in London had sent home with her.

Her days were so full she never even noticed the changes that were taking place in her body. She ate little, and slept less, but her body was swelling just the same. One early October morning, as Bernice was dressing her to go to the orphanage, Bernice let out a gasp.

"Are you with child, Lily?"

Lily automatically shook her head in denial. She couldn't be pregnant. Could she? She thought back to the day in June. "I don't think so," she said hesitantly. When had her last cycle been? She counted mentally, staring at Bernice with wide eyes.

Bernice shook her head at her. "You're thickening through the waist, and I know as well as you do, that you haven't been eating enough to keep a fly alive. Lily, who have you been with?"

Lily shook her head. "It doesn't matter." And it didn't to her. He wouldn't care that she carried his child. She looked down at herself. "Does it show?"

Bernice sighed. "Not terribly. It will soon, though. We'll have to let your dresses out, but that will only help for a short time. You're going to need to tell your brothers."

Lily felt the tears spring to her eyes. She was thrilled to be having a baby, but it would bring shame to her brothers. She needed to ask to be sent away somewhere. Not today, but soon. Very soon.

She slowly descended the stairs of the manor and knocked on the door to Charles' study. She wasn't going to hide her condition from him. He had a right to know so he could make the arrangements.

"Come in!"

Lily opened the door and took the chair across from Charles. Of the three siblings, Charles was the one who most resembled their father, but only in looks. Thank God, he didn't act like their father. "I need to speak with you, Charles."

Charles put down his pen. "Good. I needed a break from my work." He smiled at her warmly. "What do you need, Lily?"

Lily looked down at her hands for a moment. How to tell him? "I'm going to have a baby." Straight out had to be the best way. Get it over with just like swallowing a bitter medicine.

Charles stared at her in shock. He knew she'd never been alone in London, and there were no gentlemen she really came into contact with here in the country. "Excuse me?" he asked in disbelief.

She sighed. "You heard me, Charles. I'm four months along. You're going to have to send me away." She met his eyes as she said the words. She didn't want to go. She loved her work with the orphans and her life in the country. Where would he send her?

Charles shook his head. "I'm not going to send you away. I'm going to call out the bounder who did this! Who is the father?" he demanded.

She shook her head sadly. "I can't tell you that. He won't marry me, and as I love him, I won't see him dead." She played with the fabric of her dress, forming pleats and then smoothing them only to repeat the process.

"You have to tell me who it is. I'm not going to just send you away. You're carrying my nephew or niece. I wouldn't allow you to leave him anywhere, so when you come home, it'll be obvious you've given birth. What would be the point?"

"I can't tell you who it is. The man hates me. I won't be trapped in a loveless marriage." Lily's voice was flat as she said the words. She refused to let him see the extent to which the man she loved hurt her.

"You do realize that ninety percent of ton marriages are loveless, don't you?"

She shrugged. "It's not something I've ever wanted for myself. You told me I could choose my own husband. I won't be forced into a marriage." She was emphatic about that. He couldn't force her to do anything she didn't want to do.

He sighed. "You know Father would have locked you in your room and not let you out until you told him the man's name." He wasn't threatening her. He was simply reminding her how different her life was now their father was gone.

"That's why I'm so happy Father's not around to see this."

"All right. I'm not going to fight with you over this." His was filled with defeat. He wasn't willing to fight with her.

She sighed. "Thank you, Charles. For now, I'd like to go about living the way I have been. I'll continue working with the orphanage. It won't hurt anything. It's not like anyone will see me. I'll be careful." The only one who could possibly see her there would be Kit, and he already knew of her shame. What difference would it make if he knew there was a child? He hated her too much to care. She closed her eyes against the pain of that for a moment. Her father had managed to ruin her life even after his death. How could he still be controlling her?

Charles nodded. "That's fine. I'll arrange for a physician to come and examine you on Friday."

Lily nodded. She didn't want to see a doctor, but she did need to be sure the baby was growing as it should be. She also needed to start making an effort to eat more.

She stood to leave the room. Bernice was waiting for her outside the door. "Where will he send us?"

Lily smiled. "He's allowing us to stay here. I'll give birth to my baby right here in Marsgate Manor." Her voice was full of relief as she told her friend what her brother had said.

"Is he going to call out the viscount?"

Lily's mouth dropped open in shock. "I never told you the identity of the father." And she had never planned to. She'd never planned to tell anyone who it was. It was no one's business but her own.

Bernice smiled. "You didn't have to. You wouldn't have lain with a man you weren't in love with."

Lily smiled. "You do know me better than anyone." She smoothed her dress down over her rounding stomach. "I don't know how I didn't realize before today. All the signs were there." She sighed softly staring down at the slight mound that showed under her dress. "How obvious is it?"

Bernice eyed her carefully. "I don't think it's obvious at all yet. Not to anyone who didn't dress you every day. We'll let a few of your dresses out this evening, and you'll be fine for probably another month before you start showing."

"Good. Let's be off then." She indicated the front door.

"You can't be thinking to ride to the orphanage in your condition! We'll need to walk or take the carriage," Bernice insisted.

Lily sighed. "I wasn't thinking. Of course, we can't ride. I'm not taking the carriage in fine weather, though. We'll walk." As it got colder, they would have to take the carriage. She hated the idea of giving up that much of her freedom, but the baby was more important.

Bernice sighed with relief. Although she'd learned to ride over the years she'd been Lily's maid, she'd never enjoyed it. She much preferred to walk.

The walk through the woods was beautiful that morning. The leaves were changing colors and it looked as if a small child had taken his water colors and sprayed everything with them. Lily would have preferred to ride, but she found she had missed her walks through the woods. She only preferred to ride there, because it got her there faster.

The women chatted easily along the way. "Are you going to tell Mrs. Brown about your condition?" Bernice asked.

Lily sighed. "I hadn't thought about it yet. I guess I need to. She may not want me working with the children in my condition."

Bernice smiled. "Most of the children were born into the circumstance you've found yourself in."

As soon as they arrived, Lily took Mrs. Brown aside. "I need to tell you something and let you make a decision regarding the children's welfare," Lily began seriously.

Mrs. Brown's eyes widened. "What is it?"

"I'm with child. You may not want me to keep working with the children in my condition, and I would understand if you didn't. Truly, I would. I'm not exactly an example of high moral standards."

Mrs. Brown nodded. "I wondered if that might be the case. I want you here. Most of these children here came from the same sort of situation you're in. Of course, they were abandoned at birth. I assume your brother will allow you to keep your child?" Mrs. Brown knew all about Lily's situation. She and Bernice were Lily's two closest confidantes.

"Yes, and he's not sending me away to have it, either. Papa would have had a fit, but Charles just took it in stride. He's not happy with me, but he's going to allow me to keep my child. Of course, he wanted the name of the father, but I didn't give it to him."

Mrs. Brown frowned at that. "You should. Your son needs a name. Viscount Burgess will never forgive you if you try to withhold his child from him."

Lily laughed. She wasn't at all surprised that Mrs. Brown knew immediately who the father was. She'd seen the longing glances she sent Kit's way whenever he was around. "As long as the child is a part of me, he won't even want to know about it. I promise you, it'll be better if my brother never knows."

"I think you're wrong about him. You should tell him."

Lily shook her head. "I'm not going to tell him. I'm sure he'll see for himself soon enough, because I have no intention of trying to hide it from him. He hasn't made himself open to conversation." Lily rested her hand on the mound that was her growing child. She was still in shock about it being there, but was feeling more protective of it by the moment. This was her baby, and no one would ever take it from her.

That day set a pattern for the days to follow. Lily still did her share around the house, but between Mrs. Brown and Bernice, she was forced to take frequent breaks with her feet up.

When Lily protested that either of them would keep working while pregnant, they both just shook their heads. "You're a lady. You don't have to work. Let us pamper you."

Lily had been pampered her entire life. The orphanage was the only place she'd ever been allowed to do any actual work. She didn't want to be pampered.

Finally, Bernice sat down with her. "Your mother died in child birth. You need to take better care of yourself than most. I've heard of those things running in families."

After that, Lily made sure she followed their rules. She could work for two hours, but then had to take a break to sit down. The small children would sit with her and ask to be told a story or read to. She used the time to teach them their alphabet and work on beginning reading with them.

All the children became used to the frequent breaks. The older children would find chores to do while the younger children sat with Lily. The school day was an hour longer than it had been, but she found it worked well for all of them.

Chapter Six

IT WAS A FULL MONTH before Kit noticed anything different on his Wednesday visits. He had been careful to stay away from Lily, but he was on the roof, helping to patch a hole, when the older boys climbed to the roof to help. "Why aren't you in school?" he asked.

Johnny answered for them all. "It's time for Lady Lily's break. Every two hours we do chores for a bit while she rests."

Kit raised an eyebrow. Why was Lily resting every two hours? She'd never done that before. She'd always worked straight through until lunch, and then after lunch, they worked until they were finished. What was going on? "Is she ill?" he asked.

Johnny shrugged. "I don't think so. Just fat."

Fat? Lily was anything but fat. She'd always been slender. He promised himself he'd figure out what was going on once he was finished with the roof. Not because he was concerned, of course. For the children's sake, he needed to make sure she was all right.

It was lunchtime before he was off the roof and able to go into the house. He told Mrs. Brown he had forgotten his lunch, and offered to pay for a portion of the lunch she served the children. It was a lie, of course, but he had to find out what was going on.

"You will not pay for a meal. You give us so much. I wish you'd let me provide you with a lunch every day you work here, but you're just as stubborn as Lady Lily is."

He smiled at that. She was stubborn. He was glad he wasn't the only one to recognize the negative trait in her.

He took his bowl of stew and ate standing up, watching for Lily. He could hear her voice coming from the small parlor where the smaller children played during the day. He knew Lily's maid was usually the one in there with them. Instead her maid was in the kitchen helping to serve the children, which Lily had done before.

He took his bowl and wandered into the parlor. She *was* fat. Johnny hadn't lied. She was sitting on the sofa with her feet up, her meal resting on her belly. One of the smallest children was beside her eating her meal. Lily smiled down at her. She obviously didn't realize he was there.

The little girl was trying her best to imitate Lily's table manners. Lily was giving her encouragement. "Don't forget to wipe your mouth with your napkin."

Kit smiled at the picture they made before he remembered he hated her. How could he look at her and feel his insides melt every time?

"Good job. Okay. Lunchtime is over. Let's take our bowls back to the kitchen to Mrs. Brown." She set her bowl on the couch beside her and slowly got to her feet. Kit's eyes widened. She wasn't fat. She was pregnant. And she hadn't bothered to tell him.

The little girl rushed past with her wooden bowl to the kitchen. It wasn't until she was on her feet that Lily noticed Kit staring at her stomach. She wasn't going to be upset. He was bound to notice eventually.

She walked toward the open doorway he was half-blocking. "Excuse me."

He moved to fully block the door staring down at her. "You're pregnant," he said his voice low.

"I've been aware of that fact for some time now. If you'll excuse me, I need to put my bowl in the kitchen to be washed." She brought her own lunches, but she had smelled the stew Mrs. Brown had fixed and immediately handed her lunch to Mrs. Brown. "See that someone eats this. I don't want it to go to waste, but I have to have your stew for lunch."

Mrs. Brown had chuckled softly. "I was like that when I was carrying my first. It's as if your whole world is consumed by what you want to eat."

"When were you going to tell me?" he asked not moving an inch.

She shrugged. "Why would I tell you? You made it very clear that you want nothing to do with me. I assumed you would want nothing to do with my child either."

"I wouldn't if it were only your child. That's my child, too. You could very well be carrying my heir."

"Even if it is a boy, he won't be your heir. You'll marry someday, and she'll bear your child. My son will just be your bastard." The words hurt her even as she spoke them, but she didn't care. They were the truth, and there was no point denying them. "Please move aside."

"I'll get a special license tomorrow. We'll be married on Monday."

She laughed bitterly. "I'm not going to be part of a loveless marriage. You hate me. You've made that perfectly clear. Excuse me, Kit. I need to get into the kitchen." She shoved against his shoulder and he moved out of her way.

He stood staring after her for a moment. She really wouldn't marry him? It's all she'd wanted, and now she wanted nothing to do with him? She was carrying his child!

He had to think. He had to come up with some sort of plan. He wouldn't allow his baby to be raised a bastard. His child would know his father loved him in a way he'd never known from his own father.

He stalked outside to where Mr. Brown had started the back-breaking work of chopping up a fallen tree for firewood. "I need to go. I'll come and work on Friday to make up for it. I'm sorry."

Mr. Brown nodded with a smile. He'd seen the look on Kit's face when Johnny had called Lady Lily fat. Mrs. Brown had kept him apprised of the situation. Finally, the younger man was going to come up to scratch and do what he should have done months ago.

Kit saddled his horse and headed straight for Marsgate Manor. His father had been a frequent visitor there, but he'd kept his distance because of Lily. He needed to talk to Lily's brother. He'd learned as soon as he arrived home her brother was the new earl. Hopefully he would be more reasonable than his father had been.

The butler showed him into Charles's study. He couldn't recall if he'd ever met the man. His few visits to the manor after he'd come home from Cambridge had been pointed. The first, he'd been so focused on Lily, he could see nothing else. The last, he'd been so blinded by anger, he'd seen nothing else.

He strode into the room and shook hands with Charles. "I'm Christopher Burgess."

Charles smiled warmly. "I knew your father well. It's good to meet you. I'm Charles."

"Kit." He paused for a moment. He needed to get right to the point. "I need to marry your sister." There was no doubt in his mind her brother would understand immediately.

The smile faded from the earl's face. "And why do you need to marry her?" he asked savagely.

"Because I'm the father of the babe she carries," he said bluntly. The fist in his eye caused him to stumble. "I want to do the right thing."

Charles stalked him across the room. "Then you shouldn't have had relations with her before you were married, now should you?" His fist came out again, this time connecting with Kit's jaw.

"No, I shouldn't have, but I want to make it right." He refused to raise his fists to defend himself. He deserved whatever her brother dished out.

Charles sighed and walked to stand behind his desk. "I can't just keep beating on a man who won't defend himself. All right. Let's talk. Has she agreed to marry you?"

Kit shook his head. "No. But I don't think the choice is hers any longer. I think the moment she became pregnant with my child, the choice left her hands."

Charles nodded. "I agree. Here's how we'll handle it." He spoke in a low voice. "Get a special license tomorrow. I'll tell her the physician sent word her next appointment to see him was moved to Monday."

"Physician? Is she unwell?" Kit fought to keep the panicked sound out of his voice. He couldn't bear the idea of losing her or the baby.

Charles shook his head. "She's fine. We're taking extra precautions because our mother died in childbirth. I'm not risking my little sister." He paused. "Where was I? Oh, yes, you come on Monday morning with the vicar. She'll marry you then."

"Would around ten be okay?" he asked getting to his feet.

"Absolutely. Sit down. We need to talk about her dowry."

Kit shook his head. "No. I don't want a dowry. I don't need it."

Charles narrowed his eyes. "I've had a dowry set aside for her for years. You need to take it."

"I won't take it. Give it to her if you want, but I won't touch her money."

"What aren't you telling me?"

Kit sighed. "I came here four years ago. I asked for her hand in marriage. Your father laughed in my face, because I was a third son. He told me that she refused to marry anyone so far beneath her."

Charles shook his head. "Are you the man she's been pining for all these years? She never seriously looked for a husband. I wasted money on four Seasons for her, and she refused every offer that was made. Fifteen offers, and there was something wrong with every one of them. I had a feeling there was a man she wanted, but wasn't telling me about."

Kit shook his head. "No, she wasn't waiting for me. She said your father told her I wasn't happy with her dowry amount. I'm not accepting any dowry from her." He paused. "Why don't you make a trust for our baby? Or give it to the orphanage in her name? She'd like that."

Charles sighed. "That sounds like Father. He wanted her to marry a duke. He even had one in mind for her. She refused him. He lied to both of you. I hope you realize that. She said you hated her. Is that why?"

Kit nodded. "I know she didn't want to marry me once she had a chance to think about it. Why would the daughter of a rich earl want to marry the third son of a viscount? Her refusal makes sense." He stared at a spot on the wall. "I don't hate her, though."

Charles shook his head. "No, you're not listening to me. Father lied to you. She wouldn't have refused you. She's spent the past four years trying not to find a husband in London. She loved you."

"I'm sure you believe that. Thank you for your help with this." He stood. "I'd best get home and put a steak on my eye."

"I'd say I'm sorry, but honestly? I'm not. You shouldn't have touched my sister." He looked at Kit's eye and smiled. "I did a good job on it."

Kit nodded touching his tender flesh. "I'll see myself out."

Chapter Seven

BERNICE HAD TO BE LET in on the wedding plans, but she was sworn to secrecy. On Monday morning, Bernice cast so many sideways glances at Lily, she was starting to grow suspicious.

"What is wrong with you? Why are you spending so much time on my hair for a doctor's visit? He doesn't care about my hair, I promise you."

Bernice smiled. "I just thought you might want to look extra nice for a change. You're not working at the orphanage today, so I thought you could wear one of your London dresses and have your hair in a nicer arrangement than usual."

Lily sighed. "You know how much I hate it when you fuss over me forever. I thought I was done with that nonsense now we're home again." She knew she shouldn't complain, but she simply didn't want to sit still right now.

"Just humor me."

Lily sat as still as she could. Bernice hadn't put this much care into her hair since her last ball in London.

"Are you going to be going to the orphanage today? I don't want them to be left shorthanded. I really don't need you here."

"I sent Betty to take our place today. She'll take care of the young ones while the older girls help out around the house. It'll be fine." Betty usually went to the orphanage on Sundays while Lily and Bernice were at church. She also helped out while Lily and Bernice were in London for the Season.

Lily was mollified. "Thank you for that. I'm sure she'll have everything running fine." She played with the pleats on her dress. "We're going to have to let my dresses out the rest of the way within the next week. I'm getting huge."

Bernice smiled. "You look more beautiful than ever. Motherhood has put a glow in your cheeks."

Lily laughed. "Do you think I'll light up the room after dark?"

Bernice shook her head. It was nice to see Lily smiling again. She'd been so unhappy since their first day home right up until she found out she was expecting. Somehow the news that should have shattered her world had instead made her happy.

Once she was finally finished, Bernice led the way downstairs. She looked at the clock. Charles had said to have Lily in his study at ten, and it was five minutes after. Everything should be in place. "I just remembered. Charles asked me to send you to his study as soon as you were dressed for the day."

"You should have told me sooner. I wouldn't have tarried so long over breakfast if I'd known." Bernice had brought her breakfast on a tray. She didn't usually allow herself to sleep in and with the doctor coming this afternoon, it had been a nice change.

Lily hurried to the study and knocked softly. "Enter!"

She opened the door to see Kit and the village vicar. She turned to walk away. Bernice was right behind her, catching her shoulders. "Let go of me. Did you know about this?" The look on Bernice's face was answer enough. "How could you?" Lily couldn't believe she had been betrayed by her best friend and her brother.

Kit caught her hand and pulled her into the room. She looked at the Vicar. "I will not marry this man."

The vicar's eyes dropped to her expanded waistline. "I don't think you have much choice, Lady Lily." He cleared his throat and began the short wedding service.

When the vicar asked Lily if she took Kit in marriage, she refused to answer and instead stared at the wall above his head. "She does," Charles said in his deep voice.

"She must answer," the vicar replied. He looked between Lily and Kit.

Lily smiled her stubborn smile. Charles knew the look well. He looked at Kit. "I think you need to convince her."

Kit nodded, taking her hand and pulling her from the room. "You'll speak your vows." His voice didn't leave room for argument, but that didn't stop her.

Lily turned to him. "Why would I do that? You've treated me as a leper ever since we met again in June. I will not marry a man who treats me as you do."

"I will do my very best to treat you as a wife deserves to be treated," he said stiffly.

"No you won't! You hate me. There's no point. I will *not* marry you." She raised her chin obstinately.

"Lily, I don't want our baby to be a bastard any more than you do. He's just as much a part of me as he is of you. You say you love me. Do you want to deprive our child of a father's love and have him labeled a bastard for the rest of his life?" Kit appealed to her in the only way he knew how.

"Better to be labeled a bastard than to watch his father slowly kill his mother with hate."

Kit shook his head. "My house is large. We'll only see one another at meals. Please be reasonable."

"Why can't you understand that I don't want a loveless marriage?" She glared at him. "I hate the idea of being married to a man I only see at meals."

"You said you love me. It won't be loveless." He couldn't tell her he loved her. He couldn't give her that power over him, but he knew it was true. "You'll have your own room. I won't force my attentions on you."

Lily felt a tear spring to her eye and quickly dashed it away. His arguments were sound. She didn't want her child to grow up with a stigma. She loved it too much to allow that. "I don't want to live surrounded by hate," she said in a soft voice.

He wanted to tell her she should have thought of that before telling her father to tell him she wanted a title all those years ago, but he held his tongue. He pulled her against him and hugged her gently. "You won't live surrounded by hate."

She pulled back to look up at him. "Will you still allow me to work with the children?"

"Of course. Your life will stay very much the same. You'll just be living in my home instead. We'll even be bringing your maid."

"I'm not sure I'm talking to my maid right now," she said with a grin.

"Will you speak your vows?"

She nodded. "I guess I have to." She promised herself there and then she wouldn't allow his animosity to come between them.

He took her hand and led her back into the study. He nodded to the vicar. "Would you ask the question again?"

Lily's "I do" was soft, but it was there. The vicar was satisfied and moved on. Finally, he said, "You may kiss your bride."

Kit pulled her to him and lightly brushed his lips against hers, his body reacting immediately to her nearness. How was he going to be able to live with her without giving in to his need for her?

Charles came around his desk and dropped a kiss on Lily's cheek.

Lily glared at him. "I'm not speaking to you, you know."

Charles nodded. "I was certain that would be the outcome. I love you anyway."

She sighed. "I love you too, but I'm really angry with you right now."

"I know. I hope you have a happy life." He paused for a moment. "Oh, I want to tell you. Kit has refused your dowry. I've bought a parcel of land with a small house on it. You can use it as a dower house for your daughter, or give it to a second or third son. The choice is yours. He had me put the land in your name, not in his."

She looked at Kit who was talking to the vicar. He looked so handsome standing there in a suit perfect for any London ballroom. "Why wouldn't he accept the dowry?"

"Because of what Father told you about why he'd refused to marry you. He wanted you to be certain he wasn't marrying you for your dowry."

She laughed bitterly. "I know exactly why he's marrying me. For the baby. No other reason."

"He still has feelings for you, Lily. You need to help those feelings grow. Don't turn into a shrew around him. I know you're angry, too, but you have to make things work for your sake and the baby's."

"He knows I love him. I've told him often enough." She hugged Charles tightly. "I may be mad at you, but I'm still going to miss you."

"James will be angry he missed the wedding. I sent a missive to him in Scotland, but there's no way he could have arrived in time."

"I know." James had left when he found out about Lily's pregnancy. He was so angry with her for refusing to give them the name of the man; he'd left to allow his temper to cool.

"Bernice is working on packing your things now," he told her. "I'll send her over in the morning with them. For tonight, go be a good wife to your husband."

"Send her this evening, please. There's no way I'll be able to get out of this dress without her help."

Charles grinned. "That's what a husband is for, little sister. Go be married."

She didn't correct him. Of course, he'd assume she'd be sleeping with her husband. She wasn't going to tell him anything different.

She followed Kit outside to his waiting carriage. "Your maid gave me an overnight bag for you, and it's already stowed inside."

She nodded. "I was hoping she'd be coming tonight, but Charles said absolutely not. I told him I needed help out of the dress I'm wearing, but he said helping me undress was your job now. I didn't have the heart to disillusion him."

"I can unbutton the back of your dress without being overcome with lust for you," he said stiffly. He crossed his arms staring out the window, making it perfectly obvious he had no desire to speak with her.

The ride to her new home, Burgess House, only took about thirty minutes. She stared out the windows as they rode, not speaking. Her first glimpse of her new home had her smiling. It wasn't nearly as large as Marsgate Manor, and instead looked very cozy rather than imposing. The gardens were large and well-tended.

Kit helped her down from the carriage and picked up her bag. He led her into the foyer. His servants were lined up waiting to be introduced to their new mistress. She'd forgotten about this custom, and wished she could forgo it. She'd never been one to stand on formality, no matter how her father had wished otherwise.

He introduced her first to Stevens, his butler, and then Stevens introduced her to the long line of servants. She knew she'd never remember all their names, so she worked hard to commit the butler and housekeeper's names to memory, and promised herself she'd work to learn the names of the others.

Once the introductions were finished, Kit led her up the stairs. He showed her to a large room decorated in warm bright colors. "This was my mother's chamber. If there's anything you wish to change about it, just let me know."

Lily walked into the room, running her hand along the fuchsia quilt on the bed. "I'm sure this will be fine. Thank you."

Kit nodded. "I don't want anyone to know our marriage isn't a real one. Not even the servants. As far as the world is concerned, we're very much in love and you only have a private chamber because you have trouble sleeping."

"That's fine. I don't need the whole world to know that my love is one-sided. There won't be any play-acting necessary on my part. Do you think you can fool everyone?"

"Sure. I can remember back to the days when I thought you were an honest, decent person. It shouldn't be too hard." He pointed at a door. "That door leads to my chamber. If you have need anything from me, knock." He turned on his heel and left the room.

Lily sank down into a soft comfortable chair upholstered in blue off to the side of the room looking around her. It was a large open area with windows and a balcony overlooking the gardens. She could be content here. She sighed. She could be a lot more than content if her husband didn't hate her so much.

She stood and walked out onto the balcony. She knew that the huge area of woods she could see out her window led, in one direction, to the orphanage, and in another to her home. Her brother's home, she mentally corrected herself. Marsgate Manor wasn't her home any longer. She rubbed her stomach absently. "I hope you appreciate the sacrifices I'm making for you."

After a minute, she left her chamber and headed back down the stairs. She needed to at least meet with the housekeeper about menus, didn't she?

She asked the first servant she passed where the kitchens were located, and she wandered into them. The cook gave her a surprised look. "May I ask where I can find Mrs. Harding?" she asked softly.

One of the kitchen maids quickly bobbed a curtsey. "I'll take you to her." She led her off out of the kitchens. "I'm Bess. I'm sure you weren't able to catch all of our names."

Lily laughed softly. "Not at all. I learned two names, and figured I could work on the others from there."

Bess smiled at her. "I understand. We're all happy to have you here. Lord Christopher has been unhappy since returning from the continent." She paused for a moment. "We're all hoping you'll teach him to smile again."

Lily sighed. "I'll do my best." Looking around her she realized her new home was much larger than she'd realized at first. "Did you know Kit as a child?"

Bess nodded. "Mrs. Hardy is my mother. I grew up here. Lord Christopher is older than I am, but I was in my teens when he went off to war. I remember him well."

"That makes sense." She paused for a moment. "Tell me about him. I knew him a bit back then. We'd hoped we'd marry before he left, but my father refused his offer."

"He was a happy young man. His brothers were constantly criticized by their father, who was trying to turn them into whatever he wanted them to be. Lord Christopher was pretty much left to his own devices. His father wasn't nearly as interested in him as he was in his brothers what with him being a third son and all."

Lily nodded. "I'd gotten that impression."

"He probably wouldn't agree, but I think Lord Christopher was better off for being ignored by his father. His brothers were treated wretchedly." She broke off after a moment. "I shouldn't be gossiping about that. I'm sorry."

"Don't worry about it. It'll be our little secret." Lily was secretly thrilled with the information Bess had shared. It helped her understand Kit a little better. She'd need to understand him if she was going to make him fall in love with her. And she was. A loveless marriage would not work for her. She was done avoiding Kit. He was going to love her again whether he liked it or not.

Bess knocked on a door, pushing it open without waiting for a response. "Mum? Lady Lily would like to see you."

Bess backed out of the room without waiting for a response. Mrs. Harding was sitting with her head bent over a ledger sheet. She stood immediately. "How can I help you, milady?"

"First you can sit back down and call me Lily." She took the seat directly across from Mrs. Harding. "I just want to talk with you a bit about running the household. When I've been home, I've managed my brother's household for him. I want to see what I can do to make things run smoother."

Mrs. Harding looked surprised. "I hadn't expected you to take an immediate interest. What sorts of things did you do for your brother?"

"Mainly just menu planning, overseeing and hiring of servants, and other things of that nature."

Mrs. Harding looked down at her ledger. "Not ledgers then?" she asked with a slight smile.

"Oh, yes. Sometimes. I don't have a problem helping with the household accounts." She paused for a moment. "Of course, I do teach the children at the local orphanage Monday through Fridays. I can certainly help with whatever needs to be done here around that, though." She loved the idea of keeping herself busy and showing Kit that she wasn't some empty-headed bit of fluff like he seemed to think she was.

Mrs. Harding nodded. "That sounds nice. Why don't we work together on Saturdays, then? We'll do the menu planning and I'll save all the ledgers for you."

Lily smiled. "I'm not going to the orphanage today, so why don't you let me take care of that ledger for you?"

Mrs. Harding's eyes narrowed. "You don't want to spend the day with Lord Christopher?"

"He told me to familiarize myself with his home," Lily lied. She wasn't about to admit that her husband of two hours had left her to her own devices with nothing whatsoever to do.

"Well, I'm not going to look a gift horse in the mouth." She quickly stood indicating the chair she'd been using for her work. "I'll check back on you in an hour or so."

Lily stood and moved around the desk to the comfortable chair. She sat down and immersed herself in the accounts, making notes on a blank sheet of paper on ways she felt the household could economize out of habit. Her brother had made a deal with her that every dime she saved his household would go to the orphans. Maybe Kit would make a similar deal.

Chapter Eight

LILY SPENT THE REST of the day ensconced in the little room. She found the accounts were months out of date. No wonder Mrs. Harding had been so happy to hand over the task. Once they were up-to-date, she knew that a few minutes per week would keep them up.

Kit found her there shortly before seven that evening. "You didn't have to throw yourself into your duties as home manager," he said with a smile.

Lily shrugged. "It's work I'm used to doing. I've done it for my brother since my father died."

Kit pulled her chair out for her. "It's time for dinner. Are you hungry? Did you get lunch?"

Lily nodded. She knew his concern was for the child she carried and not for her, but if he felt strongly for the child, maybe his feelings for the mother would change. "Mrs. Hardy had Bess bring in a tray."

Kit led her toward the door. "Cook went all out for dinner tonight with it being your first night in your new home. He decided it should be a celebration."

She stopped short. "I need to get my shoes." She ran back to sit in the chair she'd used all afternoon, and slipped her shoes back on her feet.

Kit found himself charmed. "You never learned to wear your shoes, did you?"

She giggled. "I often hid my shoes in the carriage on the way to London balls. My aunt would make me raise my skirt to be certain I was wearing slippers, but she seldom actually attended the balls with me. She'd send me with her friends as chaperons."

Kit laughed. "And you were never found out?" He could picture her dancing at London balls with bare feet.

She shrugged. "My skirts were always full enough to hide my feet. The only problem I ran into was if a gentleman were to accidentally tread on my foot. I had to show little response. It would have given the game away completely otherwise."

"As far as I'm concerned, you may stay barefoot in the house at all times. If you can handle the cold floors, then I don't mind if you don't wear shoes one bit." He actually liked the idea. It made his wife seem more like the girl he'd fallen in love with.

He led her into the dining room where place settings were at the head and foot of a long table. They were served course after course of sumptuous food, but didn't speak again. They'd have had to raise their voices in a near shout to be heard. She was certain he'd planned it that way. She sighed. Their playful banter about her shoes had given her false hope.

By the time dessert was served, she was bored out of her mind. She played with the crust of her blackberry pie instead of eating it.

After dinner, he led her to a small library she hadn't seen yet. "I don't know if you enjoy reading, but I thought this might alleviate some of your boredom. Your maid should be here in the morning, and you'll be able to go back to teaching tomorrow."

She nodded. "Thank you." She wandered over to the shelves and looked through the volumes. She hoped there were some lighthearted novels around. She enjoyed the classics as much as the next person, but she preferred light reading when she was reading for fun.

Kit stood and watched her as she perused the books. He would have loved to offer to do something with her, but wasn't sure how to scale the wall he'd erected between them. The more time he spent with her, the more he realized that she really was what she seemed. A young woman who wanted to do everything she could for others. So why had she wanted a title so badly she'd be willing to throw away a chance at love? It made no sense.

She chose a book from the shelf. "Do you prefer all books to stay in this room, or may I take this to my chamber to read before bed?"

"Oh, do what you want with it." He glanced at the popular novel in her hand. "Are you sure that book is the type of literature a school teacher should be reading?"

She wrinkled her nose. "I like fine literature as much as the next person, but when I want to get lost in a story, a novel is all I'm after." She clutched the book to her. She had no idea how it had come to be on this shelf, but she was thrilled it was here. Perhaps one of the maids had read it and put it on the shelf when she was done. It was a rather new novel, but she couldn't see Kit or either of his brothers being interested in it.

He led her up the stairs. "Do you want me to help you with your gown now, or are you going to be up for a while?" he asked nervously. Why was he suddenly feeling so awkward? She was his wife. It wasn't like they'd never touched before. They had, or they wouldn't be in this situation to begin with.

She opened the door to her room and closed it behind him. "That would be nice," she said as she laid the book on the bed. "I don't normally dress up this much. I couldn't figure out what Bernice was up to this morning."

"Bernice is your maid?" he asked. She turned her back to him, and he swallowed hard as he stared at the long row of buttons lined up down her back. He took a step closer and put his mind to the task, carefully trying to think of anything but the beautiful woman in front of him.

"Yes, she's been my maid since I was sixteen. She's also my best friend. My father would have had a heart attack if he'd ever heard me say it, but she's only a couple of years older than me, and I've known her almost all my life."

"I'm glad you have a best friend. I lost mine in the war." It was the first time he mentioned the war to her.

She sighed. "I'm so sorry, Kit. That must have been horrible. Had you known him long?"

"We were at Eton together. The day we met, it was as if we'd known each other forever. The only other person I've had an instant connection like that with was you." Why had he admitted that to her? He needed to shut his mouth. She didn't need any ammunition against him. "There, all done."

She turned to him. "I felt that kind of connection when I first met you as well. I remember the day we met so vividly. I was just a little girl, but I remember seeing you walking through my woods, and I wanted to talk to you so badly, but I was afraid my father would find out." She used her hands to hold her gown in place against her shoulders.

"Is that why you hid in the tree?" At her nod, he smiled. "You were a sweet little thing back then. Your hair was mussed, and your dress had dirt all over it, and your bare feet were filthy. How often did you sneak out like that?"

"Oh, every day. My nanny was not an overly ambitious sort. She was always taking naps. Father figured out what was happening a few months later and sacked her. The next nanny wasn't nearly so lax. I still went shoeless whenever I could get away with it, but it was the end of my running about in the woods days." She paused and smiled impishly up at him. "After that, I had to sneak out in the middle of the night to run through the woods."

He threw back his head and laughed. He could still picture the little girl he'd been, and knew she'd have done it. "And you were never caught?"

She shook her head. "No. My nanny did wonder why my sleep habits changed so drastically, but I never told. I also learned to wash my feet as soon as I came inside. That helped a lot."

Kit leaned down and kissed her. He hadn't planned it, but she'd turned back into the woman he'd fallen in love with, and he just couldn't help himself. He'd worked hard to block the image of who she had been for so long. He couldn't fight it any longer.

She immediately moved closer into him, her arms wrapping around his neck. She raised onto her tiptoes so she could mold her body against his. She'd missed him more than she could ever express. He hadn't truly belonged to her since the day he'd left for the war. Now, suddenly, the hatred was gone from his eyes and she was going to make the most of it.

She pressed her body tightly to his, glorying in the feel of his mouth on hers. His hands started roaming over her bare back pulling her even more fully into his embrace. Her skin felt like fire everywhere he touched despite the chill in the room. His lips trailed down to the side of her neck. "Oh, Kit. I love you so much."

He froze at her words, standing up stiffly. "I'm sorry, Lily. I never meant for this to happen." He removed her arms, which were locked around his neck. He turned and was gone from the room, leaving Lily staring at the closed door between their rooms.

For a moment, she stood there her dress falling down around her hips, breathing hard. Then she pushed her dress down and off, following him into his room. He turned from where he stood beside the bed wondering why she'd followed him.

Lily marched straight up to him, and poked him in the chest. "I'm tired of you behaving this way, Christopher Burgess! I've done nothing to make you treat me badly. Nothing! All I've ever done is love you with all my heart. If you can't believe that, then I'm moving back to Marsgate Manor in the morning. I will not be rejected by my husband. You have ten minutes to make your decision. We either have a real marriage, or we have a stupid in-name-only marriage, but if that's the case, then I'm not living with you. I'd be happier at home."

She spun on her heel and left him alone, slamming the door between them. She sat in her comfortable chair staring at the clock on the mantle. If he wasn't there within ten minutes, she was going home and that's all there was to it. Their baby had a name. She didn't have to live with his idiot father.

She spun when her door opened eight minutes later. Kit stood in front of her, his cravat gone, and his shirt unbuttoned at the top. "Well? What will it be?" she demanded.

"Why did you reject me? Did you really want a man with a title? Is that why I was suddenly good enough when I came home? Because I have a title now?" He had to know the truth. He'd lived with what she called her father's lie for too long.

She stood glaring at him. "I've told you repeatedly that wasn't true. My father had a vision for each of his children. He wanted me to be the perfect lady and marry some duke somewhere. He didn't want the prestige for himself. He just thought I'd be much happier with people looking up to me the way they would a duchess." She paused. "He never understood that I would be much better suited to being a pauper's wife. I hate having to look perfect all the time. I hate having to *act* perfect all the time. I'm not allowed to be who I am."

He stood listening to her tirade not fully comprehending what she was telling him.

"I honestly liked the idea of marrying you *more* because you didn't have a title. I thought maybe we could have a small house somewhere and we could have babies, and I could go barefoot, and stop having to pretend to be something I'm not." She turned her back on him as she paced and talked. "I was honestly unhappy to learn you'd inherited the title, but I was willing to put up with it. For you. Only for you, Kit." She turned to him again tears sparkling in her eyes. "I spent four Seasons in London doing my best to not find a husband. There was only one man I was willing to marry, and he was off on the continent fighting a bloody war." She was surprised to hear herself using a swear word, but she wasn't going to take it back. She was angry and had good reason to be.

He swallowed hard, walking toward her. "You really didn't want a title, did you?"

She shook her head. "I only wanted the boy I loved who came back from war a man who hated me. I'd kept your memory alive for so long.

And you were a totally different man when you returned. Of course, I still loved you, but you didn't seem to care." The tears fell down her cheeks, and she brushed them away angrily. "I put up with the way you ignored me and made it clear you didn't care one whit for me, but I can't do that anymore. What's your decision, Kit? I'm telling you now, whatever it is, it's the final decision, because I'm not living this way any longer. You either want me in your life or you don't."

He reached down and pulled her to him, cradling her head against his shoulder. "I should have listened to you as soon as I got home. I'm so sorry, Lily. I should have believed in you the way you believed in me."

Lily sighed. She wasn't ready to give up her anger just yet. "Yes, you should have. When my father told me my dowry wasn't enough, I demanded to know what he said to you to make you leave. I never believed for one minute you'd said that." She sucked in a breath. "I always had faith in you. You should have had faith in me."

Her words cut him to the quick. "I didn't know your father like you did. I had no idea he'd lie to me about something like that."

"I should have warned you. I really thought he'd be so happy to have me off his hands, he'd accept. It never occurred to me he was set on me marrying well. I thought he'd be happy if I was married. My brother Charles explained all about his goals for me after Papa died." She looked up at him. "Does this mean you want me to stay?"

He nodded slowly, his eyes looking deeply into hers. "I love you, Lily. I'm sorry I wasted so much time."

Her face was transformed by his words. "I never thought you'd say those words to me again."

"I'll never stop saying them." He gathered her close and dipped his head for a kiss. He would never make her worry about how he felt about her again.

Epilogue

Lily climbed the stairs to her room. She'd told Mrs. Brown today, she would be willing to donate extra money to the orphanage for a teacher to be hired, but she could no longer do it. She was moving too slowly, and once the baby was here, she wouldn't want to be away from it for hours per day.

She opened the door and found Kit sprawled on her bed. (Her bed that was never used, because she preferred to share his.) He was reading a letter.

"You received a letter?" she asked with a yawn. "Who's it from?"

She sat on the edge of the chair, wanting to groan. Her whole body ached with this pregnancy. She'd been doing way too much and she needed to slow down.

He held up the letter. "Why did you never show me these? They were written to me."

It was then she noticed the box of letters at his side. The box of letters she'd written to him. Page after page of how much she hated London and wanted him to come home. How much she missed him and wouldn't marry until it was he who offered. She shrugged. "I don't know that I ever really intended you to read them after the first five or six. They turned into a diary of sorts."

He shook his head. "You know, if you'd shown me these letters back in June, we'd never have wasted all this time."

"I wanted you to trust me." Honestly, she'd never thought of using the letters.

He put the letter back in the box. He'd read hundreds of letters in the last couple of hours. "I feel like a heel. The whole time I was off hating you, you were here, pouring out your love to me. Every single day. What have I ever done to deserve you?"

She got to her feet slowly, moving slowly as she maneuvered the huge bulk of her body. She walked to the bed and sat beside him, slowly tracing his face with her fingers. "My love was a gift. You never had to do anything to deserve it, except be you."

He reached to her, slowly stroking the side of her stomach. "Thank you for a love I don't deserve." He knew then, no matter what happened, he'd spend the rest of his days in one pursuit. Loving Lily.